The School with

By: Tom Dirsa

TD Enterprises
2020

First Printing: 2020

ISBN 978-1-71600-955-6

TD Enterprises
390 Southfork Drive
Leduc Alberta Canada T9E 0E6

Photos by: Tom Dirsa

Webpage: www.tdirsa.com

Special discounts are available on quantity purchases by corporations, associations, educators, and others. For details, contact the publisher at the following email: tdirsa@shaw.ca

Dedication

This book is dedicated to all the teachers who continue to provide for their students, under trying conditions, and all the parents who continue to support their children's teacher/s.

We also dedicate this book to Ms. McNiff, our Grade 4 Teacher. Unbeknown to both of us at the time, she set me on a lifelong career as an educator.

Finally, we dedicate this book to all the individuals who contributed each and every day to the welfare of their fellow man. They are the real heroes during this crisis of a pandemic.

Acknowledgements

This book would have not been possible without the approval and co-operation of the St. Thomas Aquinas Roman (STAR) Catholic School Division and the Father Leduc Catholic School located in Leduc, Alberta. Father Leduc School represent the thousands of schools that have been closed worldwide due to the Coronavirus of 2020.

April 2020 was a difficult time to enter any school throughout the world and we were fortunate enough for our neighborhood school to agree to our proposal to take photos of a school with no students.

In particular we thank Superintendent of Schools Charlie Bouchard, Principal Tara Malloy, and Teacher Christina Mullin, who became our Ms. McNiff. We plan to donate to our local food bank the proceeds from the sale of this book.

Introduction

After being self-isolated for fourteen days we began to observe teachers working online to help their students. For those without access to the internet they began to prepare individual packets and arrange for a system of delivery and recovery.

We have observed their dedication to their students and their willingness to continue serving their students under very trying conditions. We all hope that the day when students can return to their school will come sooner than later, but until then we are convinced teachers will continue to provide, with the help of their parents, the best possible education.

In the meantime, the echo of footsteps running down a hallway or entering a classroom and the sound of voices in the lunchroom, on the playground or in the gym will remain as a memory for the staff that continue to serve their students from a distance.

This story is for all of them and hopefully will become a memory book of a time when schools didn't have students.

It's 9AM and the Hallways are

EMPTY!

Where are the Students???

It's 9:15AM and the classrooms are

EMPTY!

Where are the students?

It's 10:00AM and the Gym is

EMPTY!

Where are the Students?

It's 10:30AM and the playground is

EMPTY!

Where are the students?

It's Noon and the Lunchroom is

EMPTY!

Where are the students?

It's 1PM and the library is

EMPTY!

Where are the students?

It's 2PM and the Science Lab is

EMPTY!

Where are the students?

It's 3PM and there is Ms. McNiff, the Grade 4 **Teacher**!

Ms. McNiff where are the students?

They are all at home!

Why?

Because of the virus!

How will the students learn

while they are **away**?

We prepare lessons for them and deliver them by internet or home delivery!

Can the students learn at home?

Yes!

Teachers help them learn the lessons with the help of their parents!

When will the students return to school?

Not until the virus has been **defeated**!

Then the school will once again be filled with students and their teachers will be waiting for them!

 Tom grew up on the tip of Cape Cod in Massachusetts and moved to Alberta, Canada in 1967, for two years, which became a lifetime.

After a successful 38-year career as a teacher, basketball coach, and a school administrator he retired to Leduc, Alberta.

Since his retirement Tom began a second career as a writer. He wrote the Alberta Distant Learning Preview/Review programs for the Junior High Social Studies courses. In 2017 he was the author of **Canada Becomes a Federation** as part of the Canada Turns 150 series.

He was a free-lance reporter for the Pipestone-Flyer newspaper covering a variety of stories from city council to Rock the Rails.

For the past few years he has published a series of children picture books about a child with ADHD as he learns to cope with the world around him. They are based on his experience with his grandson who was diagnosed with ADHD.

In 2018, working with the Leduc Public Library, he published an updated history book of Leduc called **Leduc: Then & Now**.

Currently he is working on a second Leduc history book and speaking at teacher conventions.

Published Works:

Children Picture Books:
Sweaty Eyes: Published by Dream Write Publishing - November 2014
Fishing Lessons for Grandpa: Published by Dream Write Publishing - Sept 2015
BJ & the Green Monstah: Published by Dream Write Publishing - March 2016
To See a Deer: Published by Dream Write Publishing – 2018

History Books:
Canada Becomes a Federation: Published by Beech Street Books – 2018
Leduc: Then & Now: Published by TD Enterprise - 2018